Thomas
has a secret

Illustrated by Robin Davies
Series Editor: Teresa Wilson

Published in Great Britain in 2002 by Egmont Books Limited,
239 Kensington High Street, London, W8 6SA
Printed in Italy
ISBN 0 7498 5483 9

10 9 8 7 6 5 4 3 2 1

Educational consultant: Betty Root, formerly Director of the Reading Centre in the University of Reading.

"Come on, Thomas,"
said the driver.

"Come on, or we'll be late."

"I can't," said Thomas.

"Why?" said the driver.

"It's a secret," said Thomas.

"Oh come on, Thomas," said the coaches, Annie and Clarabel.

"We will all be late."

"I'm sorry," said Thomas,
"but I can't."

"You can," said the driver.

"Yes, you can," said the coaches.

"Hurry up please," said the driver.

"I can't hurry," said Thomas.

"Here comes The Fat Controller," said the driver.

"He will be cross if we are late," said the coaches.

"What's wrong?" said The Fat Controller.

"Thomas won't go," said the driver.

17

"Come on, Thomas,"
said The Fat Controller.

"I'm sorry, but I can't," said Thomas.

The Fat Controller was cross,
very cross.

"Hurry up," he said.
"You will be very late."

21

"Please tell us why you won't go," they all said.

"I'll tell you why," said Thomas, "but it *is* a secret."

"There's a bird's nest in my funnel."